Saving Our Bike Track

Story by Carmel Reilly
Illustrations by Alessia Trunfio

Contents

Chapter 1

A Gigantic Sign

It was Monday morning.
My younger brother Jerome and I
were riding our bikes to school.

The two of us ride together every day.
We follow a track from our house to school.
At the very end of the track is the town centre.

Although the track is a little rough and bumpy, we don't mind. It's fun going over the bumps. And we like riding through the paddocks and past the sea to get to school.

We were about halfway to school
when we saw a gigantic sign in a nearby paddock.
"That's new," I shouted to Jerome.
"I wonder what it's about."

We stopped and peered at the sign.

"Ocean Views Housing Estate – Coming Soon," read Jerome.
"What does that mean, Daniel?"

"I think it means lots of houses will be built here,"
I said.

"I hope our track isn't going to be covered up,"
said Jerome, anxiously.

OCEAN VIEWS HOUSING ESTATE
Coming Soon

Chapter 2

What About Our Bike Track?

Dad was in the garden when we got back from school that afternoon. We rushed to tell him about the sign.

"They're going to build houses on the paddocks!" cried Jerome.

"I heard there were plans for a housing estate," Dad replied.

"But, Dad!" I said.
"What if our bike track is destroyed?"

"Goodness," said Dad. "I hadn't thought about that."

"What can we do?" I asked.

Dad thought for a moment.
"First of all, we'll need to see the plans for the housing estate," he said.

"Is that like a map?" I asked.

"Yes, the plans will show us exactly where the roads and houses will be built," Dad explained.
"Let's call the builder and ask to look at them."

Chapter 3

Meeting the Builder

The next day, after school, Jerome and I went down to the builder's office with Dad.

The builder's name was Sara Clark.
She showed us the plans and a model of the new estate.

“It’s an amazing site, isn’t it?” Sara said cheerfully, handing Dad a copy of the plans.
“Are you thinking of buying a house there?” she asked.

“No,” said Dad. “We just –”

“We don’t want to lose our bike track,” said Jerome, boldly stepping forward.

Sara looked puzzled. “What track is that?” she asked.

“There is a track that runs through here,” said Dad, pointing to the model.
“It’s a shortcut to the school and the town centre. Daniel and Jerome use it to get to school.”

“The new houses will cover it up,” I added.

Sara nodded.
"I'm really sorry that you'll lose your track," she said.
"But this town is growing very quickly.
With more people coming to live here,
the town needs extra houses."

Chapter 4

Something for Everybody

Jerome grumbled as we left Sara Clark's office and walked back to the car.
"I don't want more houses," he said, unhappily.
"I want to keep our track."

Dad sighed. "I don't think we can save the track," he said.

But I wasn't so sure. I started to think about the track and the houses, and I had an idea.

"Can we look at the plans of the estate
that Sara Clark gave us?" I asked Dad
when we returned home.

Dad spread them out on the kitchen table.

"Do you think the track could be moved a little
so it could fit *between* the houses somehow?"
I asked.

Dad looked hard at the plans.
"Yes, I think there is space for it," he said.

"It's not just us who use that track," I said.
"Lots of people use it to get to school and town."

"And when the houses are built," Jerome added,
"there will be even more people who might want to use it."

"Yes," I said, "so it would be good for everybody
if Sara kept the track."

"Or made a new one!" said Jerome.

Chapter 5

A Brilliant Idea

The next day, we went back to see Sara Clark. I explained my idea for a new track that would wind between the houses.

"It will be good for us, and good for the people in the new estate!" I said.

"It might be possible to add it in," Sara replied, slowly.
"I'll talk to the engineers and see what they say."

Sara called Dad a few days later.
She said she had spoken to lots of people about the track.
The engineers thought it was a brilliant way
to help manage traffic.

And people who were thinking about buying houses in the estate loved the idea, too. It meant they wouldn't have to use their cars all the time.

"So, we've decided to make the track part of the estate," she said, finally.

Jerome and I are really excited about the new track.
It will be wider and smoother than the one we have now.
It will get us to school super quickly.

The only thing we will probably miss
is riding over the bumps!